ASCENT TO THE NEST

ASCENT TO THE NEST

DRAGON APPROVED™ BOOK TWO

RAMY VANCE

MICHAEL ANDERLE

DISRUPTIVE IMAGINATION

THE ASCENT TO THE NEST TEAM

Thanks to the Beta Readers
John Ashmore, Kelly O'Donnell

Thanks to the JIT Readers

Kathleen Fettig
Misty Roa
Diane L. Smith
Angel LaVey
Larry Omans
Deb Mader
Dorothy Lloyd
Micky Cocker
Jeff Eaton
Jackson Hendricks

If I've missed anyone, please let me know!

Editor
The Skyhunter Editing Team

Copyright © 2020 by Ramy Vance & Michael Anderle
Cover Art by Jake @ J Caleb Design
http://jcalebdesign.com / jcalebdesign@gmail.com
Cover copyright © LMBPN Publishing
A Michael Anderle Production

LMBPN Publishing
PMB 196, 2540 South Maryland Pkwy
Las Vegas, NV 89109

First US Edition, January 2020
Version 1.01, October 2020
eBook ISBN: 978-1-64202-677-1
Print ISBN: 978-1-64202-774-7

DEDICATION

This book is dedicated to Michael Anderle's love of Dragons in Space!

—Ramy Vance

*To Family, Friends and
Those Who Love
to Read.
May We All Enjoy Grace
to Live the Life We Are
Called.*

— Michael

CHAPTER ONE

Alex sat on her porch and listened to the passing cars. The streets were fairly empty for the middle of the day. She could hear her parents moving around nervously near the front door. Today was the day.

It had been nearly a week since Alex had finished the *Middang3ard* expansion and spoken with Myrddin and Manny. Part of her still thought the whole thing had been a dream, but after getting ready to leave this morning, she knew she was wide awake.

George and Liza opened the front door and stepped outside. Myrddin had left without restoring her sight. He said it would happen after he prepared the necessary magic, but Alex wished she could see their faces one last time before she left. She would probably be able to see them when Manny arrived, but it would be with someone watching. It was already hard enough to show them how she felt.

Liza sat down next to Alex and rested her hand on her daughter's knee. "Guess you're heading out a lot sooner than we thought you would."

Alex smiled and nodded as she squeezed her mom's

hand. "You know, I'm kinda scared. Actually, 'scared' isn't the right word. I'm terrified. I have no idea what this will be like."

George took a seat on the opposite side of Alex and lightly punched her shoulder. "You got this, kiddo. It can't be any worse than what you've already come across in the game. And besides, Myrddin said you're one of the best he's ever seen. He wouldn't want to risk you."

"It's not that. I'm not scared of any of that. Myrddin mentioned something like a boot camp when he emailed me. He made it sound like, I don't know, like a school or something."

Liza chuckled as she squeezed Alex's hand again. It was a habit she'd had since Alex was a small child, and it always made her feel like a baby. Sometimes Alex hated it, and other times, it was the most comforting thing in the world. "You afraid of finally having to go to school?" Liza asked.

Alex leaned back and turned her face to the sun, which felt amazing. "What if everyone has a problem with me?" Alex asked. "Or I don't make any friends? What if I end up being shyer than Kevin is?"

"Honey, no one could be as shy as Kevin is. That boy is hardly able to string two sentences together. But hey, even you said he's pretty popular in *Middang3ard*, so there's hope for everyone."

Alex folded her arms. She felt her face pouting and wished she was doing a better job of hiding her emotions. "I don't understand why I have to relearn everything. Myrddin said I'm one of the best that they have. What else do I have to learn?"

George stood up and cleared his throat. Alex felt like he was going to turn on "Dad Mode." It was that specific noise he used, the one that was more of a cough than an act. "You know, that might not be the best attitude to have, kiddo,"

George started. "You might want to try some humility. Just a little bit."

"I know. I know. I'm just… I just don't want to have to meet other kids, okay? It's always so uncomfortable for me. I never know what to say or who to talk to, or if I'm even allowed to talk to anyone. It'd be easier if I could just learn on my own."

"That's just because you're used to learning on your own. That doesn't mean it's the best way to do it. Besides, did you pick up all your dragonriding skills on your own, or did you get help from other players?"

Alex turned away from her father's voice. He was right, but that didn't mean she wanted to give him the satisfaction of admitting it, even though he knew already. He knew her better than anyone.

Alex heard her mother stand. "Looks like your ride is here."

Alex listened to a car roll up their driveway. It was nearly silent, so it must have been a newer model. It had to be Myrddin or Manny if her parents recognized it.

Alex reached for her mom's arm, not that she needed help to get to the car. She just wanted to feel her mother close by.

Liza and George guided Alex to the driveway as her hands trembled. She hadn't admitted to them how frightened she was of leaving. It wasn't just the prospect of being at war with the Dark One or having to learn completely new things. She was afraid of leaving her parents.

Her home had been her entire life before she found *Middang3ard*. There wasn't anyone she loved or trusted as much as her parents. Now that she thought about it, she'd rarely left the house for more than a week. The longest she'd ever been gone was on a trip with her debate team.

Manny's voice broke Alex's anxious train of thought. "Good to see that you are up and ready to go. Also glad to see you got the part about not packing anything since everything you need will be provided."

"What about friends?" Alex grumbled.

Manny harrumphed at Alex's statement. "I believe that part is up to you," the Beholder retorted snidely. "There's only so much we can offer, but I assure you that everyone in your class is about the same age. You'll at least be around peers."

George placed his hand on Alex's shoulder, and she instantly felt better. "How old are your dragonriders?"

"Alex would be one of our younger riders. Most were recruited at about the same age, but our oldest? I don't believe we have anyone over the age of..." Manny's voice trailed off before he finished. The abrupt stop meant he didn't want to complete his sentence.

Given the topic, he didn't need to. Dragonriders didn't get very old since most died in battle.

Great, Alex thought. *Just great. Dead girl walking here.*

There was an awkward silence as all four tried to figure out what should be said next. Alex already knew what time it was. This was the part where she was supposed to say good-bye. This was the part where she was supposed to leave behind everything she'd ever known.

This was the part where she was supposed to begin her adventure.

If there was ever a time for her to be brave, this was it. *They're probably freaking out right now,* Alex thought, trying to imagine what her parents must be feeling.

Alex turned to Liza and threw her arms around her. She kissed her cheek and felt the damp tears running down her mother's face. Then she turned to her father and hugged him as well. "I should get going," she said. "I'll message you guys as soon as I get a chance. I love you."

Alex pulled out her foldable cane and opened it. She

tapped it on the ground and turned in the direction of the car. Manny floated next to her. "You know, I can help you see—"

"Not now," Alex interrupted. "When we leave, okay?"

"As you wish."

Alex tapped the cane against the car and felt around until she found the door handle. She opened it and slipped inside. As she listened to the engine turn over and Manny breathe uncomfortably at her side, she'd never been happier she couldn't see. Watching her parents would have broken her heart.

Listening to them was hard enough.

CHAPTER TWO

Alex felt the car moving and assumed they were on the highway since they hadn't stopped for some time. Manny had asked a couple of times if Alex wanted him to lend her his vision, but she'd declined.

It was fairly obvious to him that Alex didn't want to talk. She'd cracked her window and was letting the cold air hit her like a hard slap across the face.

After an hour or two, the car stopped. Alex grabbed her cane, opened the door, and stepped out. She felt around for a few seconds before deciding she didn't want to start off without directions. "Manny, where are we?"

Manny, floating beside Alex, coughed quietly. "We've gone as far as the car can take us. The rest of the ride is by plane."

Alex's heart jumped into her throat. She'd never been on a plane before. Neither of her parents made enough money to travel for fun. A couple of times, Liza or George had left town for a few days, but they'd never taken Alex with them.

It wasn't a point Alex liked to bring up. Her lack of travel was a sore spot between her and her folks. She had a sneaking suspicion they could afford to take her but were afraid of how her sight might impact the trip.

Alex knew she was being paranoid. There had never been a situation where Alex's parents discouraged her from doing something because she was blind. She was just looking for excuses to be bitter.

Funny how your first feeling after leaving home is bitterness, she chastised herself.

She shifted her weight from foot to foot and tried to find the right words for what she wanted to say. She'd never been good at asking for help, not even from her parents. Asking for assistance from a floating demon-head full of eyeballs wasn't the easiest thing in the world for her.

Luckily, Manny spoke first. "Uh, is there something you need?"

"Could you guide me in the direction of the plane?"

"Are you sure you don't want to use my eyes?"

"All right, I guess it's about time. Lend me your peepers, fellow countryman!" She tried to say jokingly, but her excitement at seeing again, even if it was through his eyes, broke through.

There was a flash of bright green light, and Alex nearly stumbled from the shock. She still wasn't used to that part, but there it was: the world right in front of her eyes. Granted, it was still tinted with the odd green color she recognized from the game, but she could see.

Alex looked around at the small private airport. She'd read about how rich people could afford their own planes and assumed Myrddin wasn't any different. He *was* one of the richest people in the world, after all. People that rich didn't have time to wait at airports.

And now, neither do I, Alex thought. *Guess this must be a big deal.*

Alex pointed at the slim airplane a couple hundred feet in

front of her. "Is that the one we're going to take?" she asked, trying to make sure her voice was even and not too excited. For some reason, she didn't want Manny to realize she'd never been on a plane.

Manny floated ahead, flanked by the car's driver. "Yep, that's the one," the Beholder said. "Myrddin sent his fastest plane for you. He's very anxious to get you started on your training. He says it's imperative. You were my most important recruit all week. Jeez, I was losing sleep over you."

Alex laughed as she tried to keep up with him. For a creature with no legs, he sure as hell moved quickly. "Why were you so worried about me?" she asked.

"Myrddin was stressing me out. He kept going on and on about how I was going to lose an eye if I messed this up and terrified your parents, as if he'd forgotten how easily humans spook. Come on, we just go up the stairs."

Manny floated up the plane's staircase. Alex held her breath as she took her first step. She hadn't realized her trip to Middang3ard was going to provide so many different experiences.

The inside of the plane was decorated modestly but still managed to be luxurious. There were few seats—six at most. Each had a table, and there was a hefty amount of space between them. There was another table built into the wall, and it was set with snacks and fresh fruit.

A television hung above the counter. Alex gravitated toward it, still trying to hide her growing excitement. She chose the seat directly in front of the television and buckled her seatbelt. "We have to wear these, right?" she asked.

Manny laughed as he floated into the seat across from Alex. "I think wearing a seatbelt while flying thousands of miles in the sky is a pale excuse for safety," Manny joked. "But whatever helps you feel comfortable."

Alex smiled and looked at Manny as she reclined in her

seat and tried to find the remote. "I'm not afraid of heights. I mean, it can't feel any worse than VR, can it?"

Manny's eyes all blinked at once, causing Alex's vision to black out for a second. So, she really was seeing through his eyes. "Uh, we're allowed to watch TV on the flight, right?" she asked.

Manny was reading a dossier on his table and looked up with one of his spare eyes. "Huh? Yes, of course," he answered. "I think it only gets elvish channels, though. It's mostly news. I don't think the elves grasp the medium's potential for entertainment, although their books are spell-binding enough. Fair warning—the news of late is a little depressing, to say the least."

"Where's the remote?"

"Oh, there isn't one. It's magical. You just imagine it on, and there you go."

Manny's eye turned back to whatever he was reading, and Alex turned her attention to the television. She concentrated on turning it on, and a blip appeared. The blip slowly blossomed into an image on the screen. Alex wanted to squeal.

This was the first time she'd ever watched TV.

The image was of a thin man walking through a forest while talking to himself. There were words written on the bottom of the screen. Even though Alex didn't know what the English alphabet looked like, she knew that what she was seeing on the screen wasn't English or even human.

It was an easy conclusion since the thin man on the screen was anything but human. He looked vaguely like one of the elves from *Middang3ard*, but somehow, even through the television, he seemed more real. His skin was thin, almost see-through, yet he didn't look frail.

The elf's body looked wiry and strong. He didn't look like he was having a hard time making the hike through the woods. Alex turned to Manny. "Is this the news?" she asked.

One of Manny's eyes flipped up, and he looked at the television. "This? Yep, this is the news."

"It's just someone walking through the woods." Alex had never watched the news before, but she'd listened to it enough with her parents to know it was nothing like this. Usually, someone would explain a story.

"Elvish news is very different from human news. For one, elves don't like being lectured. It doesn't matter by who. So they've come across a more 'pleasant' way to deliver information to each other—soothing visuals with the news running at the bottom."

Alex unbuckled, then stood from her seat and walked to the television. She couldn't see much of the color of the forest. She was limited by Manny's color spectrum and the planes of vision in which he saw. But she could see that the forests were massive, sprawling things she'd never seen the like of in *Middang3ard*. "There's nothing like this in the game," she said.

"That's because the game is based on human ideas of what fantasy realms look like. In reality, each realm is much different than the next. The dwarven mines are nothing like a human could ever conceive. Not because you lack imagination, mind you, but because the dwarves are very different from any other race. And don't even get me started on gnomes. Those guys are insane."

Alex felt a rumbling from the plane. She turned her attention from the television to the window next to hers. As she walked back to her seat, she saw they were moving. Was this what her parents experienced every time they flew? This sense of adventure?

The plane rolled down the tarmac, gaining speed until its wheels lifted slowly and broke her concept of gravity. As their speed increased, the aircraft took off.

She watched all this from her window, her eyes wide as

she tried to take it all in. The airport beneath her became smaller as the plane rose, and it reminded her of being on her dragon in VR. The world around her was disappearing, leaving only the sky.

The white clouds—*Manny could see white*—rested playfully beside the plane as they sped toward a destination that Alex was all right not knowing. This was part of the adventure. Everything was a mystery right now, one she couldn't really believe was happening.

Alex pulled herself away from the beautiful vista of the sun breaking through the clouds thousands of miles above the sea. *How fast is this thing moving?* she thought. There wasn't an ocean anywhere close to where she lived. "Manny, is this plane magical too?" she asked.

Manny didn't bother looking up. He was deeply engrossed in his work. "Hm? Oh, yes," he responded. "It was enchanted by Myrddin. Sometimes we have to abide by human laws and so forth. Airspace regulations, things like that. All of it's ridiculous, but Myrddin does have a taste for fast toys and, well, you can see what I mean. Also, we are always kind of in a rush."

"Am I going to get to see any of the other realms? Like the dwarf realm?"

"Who knows. Most of our MERCs are in Middang3ard. It's something of a neutral space for the different races. Some don't like humans in their realm; they aren't as trusting. For a long time, the elves thought we were making the whole situation up. That humans were, at least."

"Don't elves trust others?"

"No, nothing like that. The threat of the Dark One was just too much for most to wrap their heads around. They wanted to pretend it didn't exist. Myrddin had to seed all of human literature with the idea of other realms, and also meet with nearly every world leader to convince them to let him launch his plan."

"What was his plan?"

"Well, you're part of it. You'll find out the details later. Until then, maybe take a nap. It's a long ride, and you're going to have a very long day ahead of you once you get there."

Alex thought Manny was more concerned about taking care of his work than helping her understand what she was getting involved with. That didn't matter though. She was ready for whatever surprises came her way.

ALEX DID NOT REMEMBER FALLING asleep, but she woke up with a start. She looked around the plane, uncertain if all of this was a dream. When she heard Manny snoring loudly, she knew it was real. Even sleeping, several of his eyes remained open, which was how she could still see. She knew she couldn't have dreamt up such an odd scene.

The pilot, who had also been their driver, exited the cockpit. He was a young man with a very square jaw and cold eyes. He motioned toward a plate of food in front of Alex. The meal was a regal porterhouse steak and a smattering of lackluster vegetables. "We've landed. Please, you should eat," he said.

Alex realized she'd never seen the meals her parents cooked her, only tasted their delicacies. She poked the steak with her fork, surprised at how squishy it was. "I'm not really all that hungry," she replied.

"It's for the trip. Myrddin would prefer it if you didn't do any realm-jumping without a proper meal. People tend to get sick."

"We're going to another realm?"

"Of course. There aren't dragons on Earth, are there? So, eat up. We're a little early."

The pilot walked back into the cockpit as Manny started to stir. When Manny's other eyes opened, he leaned over his table and began devouring a bowl of unidentifiable slop. Alex had no idea what it was and didn't want to find out.

Alex cut into her steak and took a bite. It was mouthwatering, a steak her father would have appreciated and lamented that he had not cooked himself. For the second time that day, Alex wished her parents were here appreciating this with her.

Even if her parents weren't there physically, it didn't mean they had to be kept in the dark about everything. Alex pulled out her phone, rearranged her food a little bit, and snapped a picture. Then she sent it to her parents with a message that said, **First things first. Food on plane is amazing.**

When Alex was done eating, surprised she had managed to get the whole steak down, the pilot came out and straightened his tie as he stood awkwardly. "All done?" he asked.

"One of the best steaks I've ever had. Not as good as my dad's, but still pretty good."

"Fantastic. Manny, are you ready to leave?"

Manny grumbled as he floated up from his seat, the odd porridge still dripping down his face. His tongue slipped out of his mouth and lapped up the food. Alex turned away to be respectful but also to keep from being grossed out. "Let's get going," he exclaimed.

The pilot opened the door of the plane and hit a button that caused stairs to stretch toward the ground. He led the way as they descended to the tarmac.

Once Alex was on the ground, she was able to get a better look at where she was. It was nearly night, and the light of dusk illuminated a massive facility. It reminded Alex of something she'd read about in a science fiction novel. The large white structure covered in windows seemed to glare at her with its lights.

Alex pointed toward the sprawling building. "What is this place?"

The pilot started off briskly, and Manny floated behind them. "This is the boring part of a very interesting bit of human ingenuity, mostly offices. What we're looking for is actually under the building, but I don't want to ruin the surprise."

The three of them stopped at a gate where armed guards waited. They nodded at Manny as the pilot pulled out a badge. The guards took the badge, looked at it, and handed it back. "And this is the little protégé?" the guard asked.

Alex puffed out her chest and stood as straight as she could. "I'm not little," she retorted.

"Sorry, ma'am. Didn't mean anything by it."

The guards opened the gates, and the trio walked through. There was another guard on the other side, waiting for them in a large golf cart. They climbed in and headed toward the building. Once they stopped, guards exited to guide Alex and the rest to the door.

As they passed through the foyer of the building and were guided to an elevator, Alex couldn't help looking. It was surprisingly empty, almost as if it had only been set up to look like a building on the outside.

In the elevator, Manny whistled absentmindedly as they descended. There were no floors on the display, yet the elevator continued to drop rapidly. Alex had the feeling that gravity ceased to exist for a few minutes, almost like she was in freefall.

The elevator came to an abrupt stop. It was so unexpected that Alex had to keep herself from falling. Manny snickered. "Sorry, I thought dragonriders had better balance."

Alex held onto the side of the elevator as its door whooshed open. "I'm not on top of a dragon," she retorted. "And even then, laughing is still pretty rude."

The guards didn't pay attention to Alex's and Manny's bickering as they gestured for the two to step out. Alex did as she was told and surveyed her new surroundings.

The room was massive, as if the entire area under the building had been excavated. Scientists wearing white coats shuffled around them while holding clipboards and talking hurriedly with each other. None of them seemed to notice Manny or Alex. There were no fantastical creatures that Alex could see.

Manny floated forward, with Alex trailing. They were heading toward something that was humming loudly. Alex felt like the sound was coming from inside her skull. They walked up a flight of stairs, and a few scientists moved past them. One smiled and nodded to Manny.

At the top of the steps, Alex could see why so much of the earth had been excavated. What sat in the middle of the underground research facility was nothing Alex could identify.

A long steel tube nearly thirty feet across and easily fifty feet from top to bottom stretched across the expanse. It was covered in wires and cables and ended in the middle of the facility, where something like a platform sat beneath it.

On the opposite side of the room was another metallic tube. This one was not as large, but it stretched out nearly as far and joined the other tube at the platform. The platform was small, about enough space for two people to stand on, and it had rails on all sides.

Manny continued to make his way forward while Alex stopped to watch the scientists going about their jobs. "Come on. We're kind of on a tight schedule," Manny said as one of his eyes flipped back to watch her.

Alex jogged to catch up. "Sorry, sorry," she apologized. "What is this thing?"

Manny descended the stairs in front of him. He took his place on top of the platform, and then, with one eye, he motioned for Alex to stand beside him. "This is the Hadron Collider," Manny explained.

"The Hadron Collider?"

"Yes, Myrddin had it built years ago by the Swiss." Several of Manny's eyes winked at once. "Usually, we use magic to move people from Earth to Middang3ard, but the process is complicated. Not to get too technical, but it involves binding with familiars or other creatures of magic and all other sorts of other nonsense. Since dragonriders don't have familiars, we had to figure out another way to transport people back and forth."

Alex had come across the Hadron Collider in her recent research. It sounded too unbelievable to be true, but she'd studied it simply to sate her curiosity. She'd heard the Collider had shut down and might have created an alternate reality. "Was that true?"

Manny watched as a few scientists approached them. "Was what true?"

"About the Collider creating an alternate reality. It was all in the Middang3ard chatter and stuff."

"To a certain extent. The Collider didn't create an alternate reality, it merely connected our realm to another. We had to come up with a press release. Too many people started asking why we were using up so much of Switzerland's power."

Manny laughed as one of the scientists came up onto the platform. "We're going to need you two to hold onto the rails," the scientist explained. "Once we start the Collider, there are going to be a lot of atoms coming at you very fast. We don't want you getting blown off when the portal opens."

"Is this a good idea? Getting hit by atoms?"

"Normally, no," Manny called over the hum. "But when they're magically enhanced atoms…"

Alex's mind was racing. They were going to open a portal between two different realms, which seemed impossible. But here she was, standing next to a Beholder, seeing for the second time through his eyes. Maybe the CERN reactor being a link between realms wasn't that farfetched.

The scientist walked over to a computer and checked a few readings. "All right, are you two ready?" he asked.

Manny sighed and wiped his face with one of his eye tentacles. "As ready as I can be," he grumbled before turning to Alex. "You're going to want to hold on tight for this."

Alex inclined her head toward the scientist. "I'm ready," she replied.

The man pushed his glasses up and nodded. "All right, y'all better hold onto your butts," he said before turning back to the computer.

Alex couldn't see anything happening, but she could feel it. The air around her was getting warm. The Hadron Collider started to make an odd churning noise as they turned on what she thought was the electromagnetic field she'd read about.

A sensation like gravity ceasing hit her, but stronger than when they had been in the elevator. Around her, things were beginning to blur. She realized it was because she was spinning faster than she ever had before.

There was a loud rip like paper being torn, and Alex felt the platform jerk as the world around her melted into darkness. After a moment, the black was peppered with bright lights—stars in the distance rushing toward her.

The platform continued to spin, and Alex held on with all her might as her body was pulled back and forth. Suddenly the spinning stopped, and everything went still.

Alex glanced around, but she was still too disoriented to make sense of anything.

Beside her, she heard Manny puking. "I hate that part," he finally managed to mutter.

"Where are we?" Alex asked.

"The Wasp's Nest."

Blinding lights came on.

CHAPTER THREE

A voice spoke, rich and smooth like velvet. Alex felt like the sound was melting into her ears. "I'm glad to see you made it on time."

All at once, Alex's vision, or more specifically, Manny's vision, came rushing back to her. She was in a field with greenery nearly as high as her knees. The stars shone overhead, and there was a strong, chilly breeze rustling the grass.

Alex jumped back when she saw a griffin standing in front of her. She nearly screamed before her eyes widened with a level of awe she hadn't known she was capable of feeling.

The creature had broad, deep-brown wings that stretched nearly ten feet. Its towering lion's body was covered with majestic golden fur that seemed to catch what little light was cast by the moon.

The griffin bowed so deeply that its eagle's head almost touched the ground. When it rose, it looked as if its beak were turned up in a smile. "You must be Alex," the griffin said. "My name is Samara. I'm pleased to meet you."

Alex held her hand out from habit, and the griffin looked

curiously at her. "Uh, I'm Alex. I'm pleased to meet you as well. Um, where are we?"

"Outside the Wasp Nest. It's complicated to teleport into an enclosed space, but we aren't far. Manny, will you be coming as well?"

Manny had stopped floating and was lying on the ground. He still looked very sick. Most of his eyes were half-closed as he moaned loudly. "I'll be coming," he groaned. "Just give me a minute. I think I'm going to be sick again."

"You should probably get up if that's the case. I'd hate to see how that turns out if you're lying down."

"Right, right," Manny said as he righted himself and floated back into the air, still trembling. He looked like he could puke at any moment, and he burped loudly. "Just give me a sec."

Samara turned her head toward the sky, her beak still casting the illusion of a smile. "The wind is beautiful tonight, isn't it?" she asked. "It's been so warm here that I didn't think we were ever going to get a nice, breezy night. Perfect night to stretch my wings. I'm glad you both came."

Alex hadn't been able to take her eyes off Samara's wings. As she spoke, the griffin stretched and flexed them in the same way some people gesture with their hands when they talk. It was elegant and transfixing; Alex felt as if the griffin were telling a story with each flourish of her feathered appendages.

Samara ruffled her feathers as she knelt and turned her right wing to Alex. "While Manny is getting his bearings, why not hop on?"

Alex's heart had jumped into her throat. Was she already heading to the air, even before she got to ride a dragon? This was the best decision she'd ever made. "You mean, we're going to fly?" she asked.

"Oh, goodness, no, little one. I'm sorry, I hope I didn't get your hopes up. I don't take humans into the air, especially humans who still have to go through their training. I mean no disrespect. You were no doubt an amazing rider in *Middang3ard* VR; otherwise, you wouldn't be here."

"So, how come you don't let humans ride you?"

"Well, just not any human. Riding a griffin takes a purity of heart that the average human doesn't have, at least when we're in the air, but you will get to ride on my back for a quick sprint. I warn you, though; I refuse to have reins placed on me. You're going to have to hold on very tight. Climb aboard and let's get going."

Alex was disappointed and instantly felt silly about it. She was about to ride a griffin to her new dragonriding training program, and she was feeling slighted by not being able to ride the griffin into the sky? *Now that's being childish,* Alex thought.

Alex climbed onto the griffin, using its wing as a ladder, trying not to hold onto it too tightly or pull out any feathers. The griffin chuckled as it watched Alex struggle to get aboard. It was a wholesome laugh that reminded her of her father's.

Already, Alex could tell the difference between VR and the real Middang3ard, if that was in fact where she was. Hardly any of the dragons or magical creatures in-game ever spoke, and those that did lacked the personality of Samara. Alex hadn't even thought about the fact that she was talking to a living, breathing creature. It just seemed natural that Samara would speak.

Once Alex and Manny were both on Samara's back, the griffin took off. Alex wracked her brain to try to understand how Manny was holding on without legs or feet but she grabbed Samara's fur as tight as she could.

Samara bounded through the darkness. She was faster than anything Alex had ever ridden, in-game or out. When

Alex was younger, her parents had taken her to an amusement park. She couldn't get enough of the rollercoasters, and she hadn't thought she'd ever ride anything that fast again in her life.

Alex was wrong. She was barely able to maintain her grip as the wind beat against her face and pulled tears from her eyes that she tried to beat back by blinking. When she looked at Manny, she could see several of his eyes were closed, and he still looked sick to his stomach.

Up ahead, there were thousands of lights. Their destination looked like it had a landing pad. There were crystal structures that reflected and refracted the lights, so it appeared as if there were solid rainbows coming out of the ground.

The buildings ahead reached toward the night sky, stretching and curving as if they were made of water. It was the most beautiful thing Alex had ever seen. If she strained her eyes, she thought she could see people walking through different parts of the crystals.

The closer they got to the Wasp's Nest, the more details she could make out. There were crystal bridges between many of the columns. She couldn't quite see through the building, but she could see shadows moving around in the rainbow structure.

Samara ran up to a bridge that stretched over a crystal-clear moat. The water smelled divine, and Alex wished she could have slipped in for a swim. There was a chilly breeze, sure, but Alex had always been a fan of cold night-swims.

Past the bridge, Samara stopped at the gates of the Wasp's Nest. There was something regal about the way they stretched up, almost like a drawbridge. Alex felt like she was walking into a medieval play of some sort, a heroine atop her magical griffin.

There were two guards at the gate and seeing them

completely pulled Alex out of the medieval fantasy. Each was human and heavily armored. Their vests looked like Kevlar, and their helmets had holographic visors.

Rifles were slung over their shoulders. They were not the sort Alex had heard described before. These reminded her of something out of a science fiction movie. Tubes and wiring were incorporated along the rifles' steel barrels and synthetic grips.

One of the guards lowered his gun when he saw Samara. The other didn't bother but grew noticeably more relaxed. "Oh, it's just you," the first guard said. "I didn't know you were going out for the night."

Samara spread her wings and leaned slightly to the side, so one of her wings touched the ground. Alex took this as a sign that she was supposed to get off Samara's back. "I was picking up our latest resident, the new *human* dragonrider." The way Samara said "human" revealed to Alex that her species was what was causing the stir, not that she was a great VR rider.

The guard on the left stood up a little straighter and pushed his visor up. He peered at Alex with steely blue eyes. "A human. We must be desperate if we're recruiting humans."

"Nothing of the sort. Myrddin has merely been trying to add to the roster. We can't be overprepared for the Dark One. Underestimating him might be what causes us to lose this war, and we've already lost so much."

The guard nodded as he reached toward the gate. The crystals in front of him contorted and stretched to form a panel. He typed in a code, and the panel dissolved back into the wall. The double gates of the Wasp's Nest opened, and a nearly blinding light shot out.

Samara led the way and Alex followed, trying not to stare at the armed guards. She'd been expecting something a little more like the game *Middang3ard*, not a military thriller.

What she saw once she was inside the Wasp's Nest was even more surprising.

The gates opened into what at first looked like a lobby. Upon closer inspection, it seemed the room was some kind of information hub. The walls were sweeping Victorian architecture, with crystal columns stretching to the domed ceiling

People were walking through the large room, hardly noticing each other. Everyone seemed extremely busy. *I wonder what's going on?* Alex thought.

As Alex watched the people and sped up to catch Samara, she noticed almost no one around them was human. Most were elves, but there were also dwarves she wanted to stop and stare at. It was almost impossible to tell the male dwarves from the females. Both had ludicrously long and thick beards, and all wore heavy leather studded armor that contrasted with the sweeping robes of the elves.

Alex looked around, letting her eyes drink in everything they could. Samara stopped and looked back at Alex, smiling with her eyes. "First time seeing anything other than a human, right?" the griffin asked.

Alex turned back to the griffin, hardly able to contain the joy on her face. "Yeah, no kidding!" she exclaimed. "I didn't know...I didn't know there were so many of them!"

"I would have thought you would have been more surprised to see a majestic griffin than an elf or a dwarf. I am, in fact, a beast of legend."

Alex was preparing to apologize until she saw that Samara was still smiling. It had been a joke, but that didn't mean Alex couldn't explain herself. "I was surprised when I saw you," Alex began. "But you're so different from everything else. I almost can't believe you're real."

Samara winked at Alex. "Flattery will get you nowhere," she said as she turned away. "Come. We don't want to keep

Myrddin waiting. He wanted to speak to you in person after you arrived."

"Is Myrddin always here?"

"No, rarely, actually. Most of his talents are useful in other places. I and a handful of others run the Wasp's Nest. It would be a mistake to expect Myrddin to be here. There is too much for him to do; too much for all of us to do."

Samara guided Alex and Manny through the throng of elves, dwarves, and halflings walking around the crystal lobby. They passed a desk where a beautiful elvish woman with long, flowing silver hair was helping a disgruntled gnome who was standing on the desk, gesticulating wildly.

Alex was glad to see people behaved ridiculously, regardless of their races. She continued to follow Samara through the throng, and they paid her no attention despite her open-mouthed gawking.

Samara turned left at the end of the room, and a crystal hallway seemed to appear out of nowhere. As Alex walked, she looked at the ceiling. Even though she was still seeing through Manny's eyes and there wasn't much color, she could make out different hues shimmering above.

If there was anything like walking through a rainbow, this was it.

As they continued down the hall, Alex noticed there were doors on either side of her. She couldn't see through any of the crystal doors, but she could see shadows and figures moving behind them. It gave the impression that the Wasp's Nest was alive.

She understood where they'd gotten the name since the whole place felt like a giant hive. She shuddered, thinking of the mountain hive she'd braved in *Middang3ard* to get here. This was considerably better. "Nest" was a much more appealing moniker than "hive."

Samara stopped in front of an elevator at the end of the

hallway and reached toward its doors. A panel pushed out of the crystal, and Samara pressed her talon to the pad. The pad binged loudly, and the doors of the elevator opened.

When the three stepped in, Alex was surprised to find that the elevator was so roomy. It didn't look like there was going to be enough space at first, but now she was certain they could have fit in another griffin if they'd needed to.

The elevator descended with a whoosh right after the doors glided closed. She looked at Manny, who had been bizarrely quiet. When she saw his face, she knew why. The Beholder looked ready to puke again and was slumped against the wall, only a few of his eyes open.

Alex leaned over to Samara and whispered, "Do you think he's going to be okay?"

Samara gave Manny an accusatory look. "Oh, yes, he'll be fine eventually," she assured Alex. "Beholders have trouble traveling through realms in ways they're unaccustomed to. Magic is their preference, and technology tends to make them…well, you can see how Manny looks for yourself. He's being a baby about it, as usual."

One of Manny's eyes whirled and glared at Samara. "I'm not being a baby," he grunted. "I just don't have as robust a constitution as you. Most of my insides are just gunk and organs. I don't even have a bone structure to help deal with all that gravity, so thank you for your sympathy."

Samara leaned over and nipped the back of Alex's ear lightly. "I just like to give him a hard time," she whispered. "He's always so proper, but when he's sick, he's like a little kid."

The elevator came to an abrupt stop and the doors slid open. Samara stepped out and motioned with her head for the rest of them to follow.

The lower section of the Wasp's Nest had a completely different look to it. Everything was still made of crystal, but it was no longer clear. The walls were black, and there were far fewer people milling about. Most of what Alex could see was split into offices. There was a loud hum coming from above.

When Alex looked up, she saw dozens of people zooming around on what appeared to be hoverboards. She couldn't get a good look, but she knew technology like that didn't exist on Earth yet.

Hoverboards might have been a huge surprise to Alex, but she was starting to put things together. It would only make sense that Myrddin and his task force didn't only rely on magic. They would have to use technology as well. It would be ignorant not to.

Samara guided Alex and Manny down some stairs to the front desk where a ruddy-faced gnome was sitting. He looked up from a pile of paperwork, barely able to see over it. He grunted as he jumped off of his chair and climbed onto the desk, where he stood beside the pile of paper. "It's good to see you," Samara brayed.

The gnome crossed his arms and leaned against the pile, nearly knocking it over and falling off the desk before catching himself. "It's nice to see you too, Sam," he exclaimed. "This the new kid Myrddin got his undies all bunched up over?"

"There are more polite ways to say that."

The gnome shrugged and pointed at a room on the left. "Waiting for you in there," he said. "I'll forward the paper-work to you." The gnome pointed at the pile of paper. "I ain't going looking through that right now."

The gnome jumped off the desk and returned to his chair, where he reached as high as he could, snatched a piece of paper off of the pile, and got back to his work. Samara held her head up high as she walked away from the gnome in the direction of Myrddin's office.

As Alex followed, she noticed that the room she was in was changing slightly before her eyes. The crystal walls were stretching and rearranging themselves. They flexed as if they were considering the needs of those passing by. It was a beautiful thing to watch.

Samara finally reached Myrddin's office. There was a modest door with an even more modest plaque that read Director. Samara knocked on the door and Myrddin's voice from within said, "Come in."

The door opened of its own accord. Alex noticed that this door seemed much less modest as it stretched, nearly too quickly or too perfectly to be seen, to accommodate Samara.

Manny followed Samara, and the door became the same size as Manny's body. Alex went last.

Myrddin's office could best be described as books in need of more space. Every corner of every wall was covered in shelves, which in turn were covered in books. Alex assumed Myrddin was sitting at a table. If not, he'd managed to find a way to float books perfectly still in front of himself for decoration.

Myrddin looked up from a large, ancient-looking tome and smiled when he saw Alex. He closed the tome, and a puff of dust shot up from its pages. "Oh, it's good to see you've finally made it. I was starting to get worried about you three," Myrddin said as he waved his hands.

The books on the table flipped upright and zoomed across the room to their proper places in the bookshelves. As the rest of the books started to dance around and move, Alex saw chairs next to the door. When she got a chance, she took a seat.

Alex shifted slightly as Myrddin watched her. "This place is beautiful," she exclaimed. "What exactly is it?"

Myrddin looked around at the crystal room as it seemed to breathe. "The Wasp's Nest?" he asked. "Oh, a little creation of mine—a perfect balance of magic and technology developed specifically for breeding dragons and housing our riders. One of my greatest inventions."

"I didn't know you used so much technology."

Myrddin nodded as he scratched his beard. "Yes, a common mistake. Authors have seeded Earth with tales to make accepting the fantastical more palatable, but few people have picked up on our work in science fiction as well. James Cameron was one of my leading agents. There were many avenues we had to go down to prepare folk for the coming of the Dark One."

"What exactly is the Dark One?"

"All the horrors from every story you've ever heard wrapped up in one very dark and evil package."

Myrddin waved his hand again, and everything in the room vanished. Instead, Alex was floating in space above Earth. There was a massive meteor shooting toward them. "I don't know how yet, but this is the Dark One's doing. We need to intercept it, hence…"

The darkness of space broke apart, as did the crystals of the room. Everything warped and changed around Alex. When the crystal reset, she was standing in a large room. A dragon was strapped to something like a chair before her. Elvish scientists were attaching cannons to the dragon's shoulders and installing technical modifications on its body.

The dragon looked very annoyed.

Alex took a step back as she gasped in awe. A real dragon, right in front of her. She could smell the sulfur coming from its nostrils.

The dragon turned its eyes to Alex and sighed loudly, emitting a blast of heat as one of the elvish scientists tried to wave away the beast's breath.

Alex stared at the dragon. It was so beautiful she almost

couldn't speak. "That's…that's what I'm going to be riding?" she asked.

Myrddin walked over to Alex and patted her on the shoulder. "Eventually. We still need to get you trained."

Alex's brain snapped back to the practicalities. "What about my eyesight?" she asked.

"I'm working on it. Trust me, we can't have you on top of a dragon with Manny sitting behind you."

"Well, what do I do until then?"

"We start your training immediately. Samara, take Alex to get suited up."

CHAPTER FOUR

S amara led Alex down a series of changing crystal hallways while Manny slunk behind them, still fighting his nausea. Alex was enamored of the changing crystals and didn't notice the griffin had stopped walking. As Alex continued forward, she bumped into Samara's raised wing. "Oh, sorry," she muttered.

Samara smiled with her knowing eyes and chuckled. "It's okay. Everyone is enchanted by the Nest their first day. But here you are, ready to be fitted." Two doors ahead whipped open, and Alex jumped at the sight of what was behind them.

An ancient-looking creature that was a combination of human and snake, the worst parts of each, stood before Alex. It had six hands, each holding a device Alex had never seen. Some looked like advanced guns and others like knives. It hissed loudly when it saw Alex.

"Get down," Alex shouted as she pushed past Samara. She looked around for a weapon. A few feet away from the creature was a table with another of the knife-like objects the beast was carrying. She dove into the room, scooped up the weapon, and brandished it at the monstrosity. "I won't let you hurt my friends," she shouted.

The snake-like creature hissed again and slithered around Alex while Samara burst out laughing. The creature continued past the new dragonrider and wrapped its arms around Samara's neck as the two nuzzled each other. "It's been too long since you stopped by, Sam," it rasped.

"What? What?" Alex started.

"That's a naga," Samara replied casually.

Hearing Samara's calm tone, Alex put her weapon down immediately and tried to hide how embarrassed she was.

The naga turned to Alex and extended one of her empty hands. "You must be the new recruit. Glad you have some fire in you. My name is Primerose. I appreciate your enthusiasm, but you're gonna have to learn an important lesson very quickly. Just because it looks scary, that doesn't mean it's evil."

Alex hung her head as she tried to back away and get close to Samara. "I am so sorry," she apologized. "The only time I've ever seen—"

"Was in *Middang3ard*, right?"

"Yeah. That was what I was going to say."

"The real world of Middang3ard is much more complicated." Primerose turned to Samara. "Thanks, Sam. I'll take it from here. And stop ignoring my lunch requests. I know we're all busy and—"

Samara raised one of her talons and cut Primerose off. "Understood. Tomorrow, I promise," she said as she lumbered gracefully away.

Primerose turned her attention back to Alex and ignored Manny, who had chosen to move to a corner where he could sulk undisturbed. "All right, now we have to get you outfitted," Primerose said, her many hands moving around, their tools shining brightly in the crystalline light.

Alex took a deep breath and stepped closer to Primerose. "What do you want me to do?" she asked.

"Well, first, I have to get you measured."

"For what?"

"Your suit. I do all the outfitting for the dragonriders and the dragons."

"You mean, like what they were putting on the dragon earlier?"

Primerose flashed Alex with what looked like a rectangular flashlight. An energy grid displayed on Alex's body, displaying a multitude of numbers and signs Alex didn't understand. "Exactly. I do the measurements and prepare the information," Primerose said. "I usually only apply the suits to cadets, though."

The energy grid disappeared, and Primerose turned to a computer terminal behind her as her other hands continued to move around Alex. "You said that things were more complicated on Middang3ard than in the game," Alex said. "What did you mean by that?"

Primerose glanced at Alex and smiled sweetly. "Oh, it's very complicated. Things are black and white in the game to help with the narrative. In real life, not everyone is on the side you assume. Take the drow, for example."

"You mean the Dark Elves?"

"You should keep in mind not to call them that. It's practically a racial slur here, but yes. The drow in-game are bad antihero-types. In real life, they all have their own needs, their own desires, and nearly all stand against the Dark One."

Primerose moved back toward Alex and her hands started to measure things all over again. It was too fast for Alex to see what they were doing, but she didn't miss the result. Primerose was starting at Alex's feet and working her way up, stitching armor straight onto her body. "Even the dragons are complicated." Primerose sighed.

Alex's attention was piqued by the mention of the dragons. "What do you mean, the dragons are complicated?" Alex asked. "I thought dragons were pretty straightforward creatures, kinda like Samara. Griffins are always regal and dignified. I thought dragons were the same."

"Oh, don't get me wrong. They are very dignified, just not all on the same side. We assumed all the dragons would want to stand with us against the Dark One. We were wrong. There are some dragons on the Dark One's side, even one golden dragon."

Alex couldn't believe what she was hearing. Golden dragons were the epitome of dragon purity. It was said they were born of the alchemical gold in the veins of the earth. They were creatures of great integrity and compassion, wiser than the other dragons.

Primerose was now working her way up Alex's midsection. The armor she was being tailored into fit as snug as another set of skin. It was lightweight and seemed to stretch with every one of her movements. "How can that be?" Alex asked. "Aren't gold dragons… Aren't they kinda the best?"

"Forget all that stuff you've read about dragon hierarchy, kid. It doesn't really work like that. Sure, that's what people say, but trust me, I've worked with a lot of dragons, and all are trying to make their own destiny. Raise your arms. We're almost done."

Alex did as she was told and Primerose continued, stretching the fabric over Alex's arms and chest, working her way up to Alex's neck, coming back to her hands, and ending at her wrists. Once done, Primerose smiled as she pulled out what looked like a gun.

Alex sucked in a deep breath as her body tensed. "What's that?"

Primerose looked at the tool and smiled as she shrugged. "Oh, this? It's the last step. Still gotta give you your dragon anchor," she explained. "Ties into the rest of the suit. It's mostly tech, very little magic. Made to survive nearly any atmosphere or climate. Don't try flying into the sun, though."

"So, I'll be tied to a dragon?"

"That part's still coming. There you go. Go ahead and take a look."

Primerose moved to the side so Alex could see herself in the full-length mirror. Her outfit really was like a second skin. There was no bulk, unlike the armor she'd had in-game. There were electrical nodes on her shoulders, spine, and kneecaps.

Alex turned and admired Primerose's handiwork. "It looks great!" she exclaimed.

Primerose went over to the desk and grabbed two nodules, which she pressed to Alex's temples. "There you go," she said. "Those are for your HUD. You'll find out about that later. Now we gotta get you going. I think the rest of the recruits are having chow about now."

Primerose shooed her out of the room as Alex tried to catch one last glance of herself in the mirror. Once Alex was out the door, she turned and nervously picked at her knuckles. "I'm really sorry about earlier," she murmured quietly. "Really sorry."

Primerose slithered over to Alex and kissed her forehead. "Don't worry about it," Primerose hissed. "You've got killer instincts. Now get out of here and get some food. If you need anything, don't hesitate to ask ol' Rose, all right?"

"Gotcha!"

Alex turned as Manny slowly floated ahead. "Come on," he said. "I'll take you to the mess hall."

Alex heard the doors to Primerose's studio shut as she followed him. The sheer excitement was almost too much for her to hold in. She kept looking down at her dragon anchor. This was really happening. What was next?

CHAPTER FIVE

Manny and Alex made their way down the winding corridors of the Wasp's Nest. The allure of the crystals changing around Alex had not worn off, but she was already getting used to the magical tech of the place ebbing and flowing. It was comforting, like being hugged.

Manny seemed to know his way around, so Alex followed him, content to be lost in her thoughts without worrying too much about the Beholder. She wondered how different riding a real dragon was going to be.

Already, meeting creatures of other races was not what she had expected. Samara, the griffin, was much more down to earth than Alex would have guessed. Everything she'd read about griffins emphasized their royal, perhaps even haughty, nature. Samara was anything but.

The same could be said of Primerose. Anytime Alex had come across a naga in the game, it had been an enemy, something that needed to be defeated. Primerose was one of the sweetest people Alex had ever had the joy of meeting. After the brief period of time they'd spent together, Alex felt like she could tell Primerose anything.

And then there was Manny. Beholders were ancient creatures who had been born at the beginning of time and possessed ancient knowledge. They had grown bitter toward the worlds they'd watched grow old around them.

Manny seemed like a slightly disgruntled paper-pusher. Definitely not the thing of nightmares she'd heard Beholders were supposed to be. If Manny was an eldritch creature, she wondered what the rest were going to be like. Manny reminded her of a grouchy, well-meaning uncle more than anything else.

The two turned a corner and Manny stopped, causing Alex to bump into him. One of his eyes swung back and stared at Alex. "Oh, sorry," she said. "I was caught up in my thoughts. You know, all the new stuff."

Manny spun around, smiling for the first time since the two of them had gotten off of the plane. The color had come back into his face, and he was the picture of perfect health—or at least, Alex assumed this was what a healthy Beholder looked like. "Don't worry about it, kid," he said.

Alex stared long and hard at him. Even though he did look like he was in a better mood, there was still something off. He looked like he might be nervous or keeping a secret. "Hey, Manny, what's going on?" she asked.

Manny flipped one of his tentacles in the direction of the cafeteria. "Just wanted to give you a few words of encouragement," he finally said. "We're about to step into the real Wasp's Nest. The mess hall is where all the dragonriders go to blow off steam."

Alex shrugged as she tried to peek around Manny's shoulder. "Okay, so what's the big deal?" she asked. "It's just a bunch of people."

"I mean, well, people can be very cliquish. You got your vets, who tend to only talk to other vets. And you got your recruits. A lot of them have already split into the parties they think they're going to be with."

"What does any of that have to do with me?"

"I'm not going to say this is going to get as advanced as office politics or anything like that. Myrddin just mentioned that, you know, you haven't done the whole high school thing. I'm just saying, don't let anyone get under your skin. Especially if they're trying to."

Alex nodded as she crossed her arms and smiled. Manny did sound exactly like an uncle. "Yeah, no problem," she assured Manny. "I've got pretty tough skin, and it's not like I've never been around anyone my own age. I'm not some sheltered hermit. I think I'll be fine."

Manny floated toward the door as he turned away from Alex, one of his eyes still over his head so he could watch her. "Don't say I didn't warn you," he cautioned. "You know how they say kids are cruel? That doesn't have anything on the cruelty of teenagers. Rivals the Dark One himself."

The cafeteria doors opened for Manny, and he practically flew in before stopping himself abruptly. "Also, you need to stay kinda close to me. There's only a certain range I can provide you with my sight. If you go too far away, you'll lose it," he explained.

Alex sighed loudly, hoping Manny could hear her, then instantly regretted trying to make Manny feel bad. "Well, how am I supposed to get to know anyone if I have to stay right next to you?" she asked. "I assume you don't want to hang out with a bunch of high schoolers."

"Actually, I couldn't care less who you're sitting next to, but I'm going straight for the food. I'm starving. There's not really a whole lot of food in me right now. So, let's hit the chow line, and then I'll just follow you. Also, don't bother trying to talk to me while I'm eating. Trust me."

Manny was already in the mess hall, so Alex followed

him. She wasn't sure what she'd been expecting. She'd read about military mess halls and school cafeterias and had worked out the rest in her imagination. This was nothing like that.

There was a large crystal fountain in the middle of the room, spouting the clearest water Alex had ever seen. A statue extended from the fountain, depicting an elf, a human, and a dwarf crouched beneath a dragon on its hind legs, breathing fire.

The fire was captivating. Even though it was made of crystal, it must have been enchanted to give the illusion of real fire. Alex almost thought she could feel the heat coming from it.

Around the fountain, there was a lush garden with benches spread gracefully throughout it. A variety of folk occupied them, intermingling with each other. Alex couldn't see any rhyme or reason to who sat with who. None of the races seemed to be keeping to themselves.

Alex leaned over and nudged Manny. "Which ones are the recruits, and which ones are the vets?" she asked.

"Oh, recruits are in gray and white, and those who've passed their courses are in black and red. Now, keep up. I need to eat!"

Manny wasn't kidding. He took off to the right as soon as the words were out of his mouth. Alex had to jog to stay with him. She tried not to get distracted by everything going on in the room but didn't do a good job of it.

As Alex tried to keep pace, she saw a ball flying through the air. A small group of pixies zoomed past, chasing the ball. The pixies left a trail of bright light behind them, and Alex wished she could have gotten a better look at them.

Suddenly, the world around Alex started to scramble the way a television flickers when it's losing its signal. Alex instinctively reached for something to hold onto. Her hand found a rail on the wall. "Manny," she shouted, a little too loudly.

Her vision righted itself just in time to see a group of people about her age staring at her, obviously annoyed at her outburst. Two pairs of eyes stood out. The first belonged to a drow boy. His skin was as dark as midnight, and his eyes were a deep purple.

The second pair of eyes were those of a gruff-looking gnome. Alex couldn't tell how old the gnome was due to the scruffy beard that obscured most of his face. All Alex could see were his pitch-black eyes staring from underneath a mass of white hair.

Manny came floating over to Alex. "Sorry, I thought you were right behind me," he said. "Come on." Manny took Alex's hand and guided her to the lunch line on the right side of the room.

Alex didn't need Manny to hold her hand, but she appreciated having someone familiar to ground her. Even though she'd gone her entire life without seeing anything, she'd already begun to rely on her eyes. The brief moment her vision disappeared had been more unsettling than the first time she could see.

The lunch line looked more like what Alex had read about but much fancier. It reminded her of the time her father had gotten a promotion, and they'd gone out to a fancy brunch restaurant to celebrate.

There were rows upon rows of buffet-style dishes floating in the air, with a magical flame floating beneath each. Next to them were trays.

Manny quickly moved around, grabbing whatever he could get his tentacles on and piling it on his tray. Alex took a little more time as she looked at each of the dishes. She hardly recognized any of them. Each dish had a tag that stated which race it was a delicacy for.

Alex wanted to try one of the elvish dishes, but at the same time, she really needed something familiar. The look the drow boy had given her had left her shaken. There was something in his eyes she didn't quite understand.

A plate of mashed potatoes and fried chicken was going to have to do. She grabbed her food, went over to a beverage-dispensing machine, and was once more overloaded by the number of options. She chose cola to make her life simpler.

Manny arrived beside Alex, already shoveling food into his mouth. "All right, where do you want to sit?"

Alex looked out over the sea of people talking to each other over their meals. *Yeah, this is going to be easy*, she thought.

CHAPTER SIX

Alex wandered around the mess hall, trying not to spend too much time staring at the different groups of people. Instead, she focused on the magical and technological wonders around her. She stopped near the fountain and marveled at the garden growing around it.

The garden was filled with flowers that bloomed in colors that almost put the rainbow of the crystal ceiling above to shame. Alex couldn't tell exactly because she was seeing muted color through Manny's eyes, but he let her know that the true sight of them was beautiful.

Alex didn't feel like she was missing out. She could smell the aromas of the flowers. Some of them reminded her of home, and others were vaguely reminiscent of scents she'd caught in *Middang3ard* but were stronger here.

Manny floated away from Alex, giving her space as she stared down at her plate. She knew she was going to have to reach out to someone. No one ever approached the new kid, according to teenage literature.

Alex finally forced herself to look up. The drow and gnome who had heard her shout earlier were sitting within earshot, and both were staring at her. Neither said anything, but as they turned to look at each other, the drow sneered while he pointed in Alex's direction.

She ignored the obvious snub and turned to see what else was going on. Even though she was trying to put on a brave front, her insides were squirming. She felt like her neck was very hot, and she had the odd desire to walk around.

A ball flew over Alex's head. She instinctively yelped and ducked. A few feet away, the gnome and the drow snickered, not bothering to hide that they were laughing at her. Above Alex, the pixies chasing the ball zoomed by.

One of the pixies abruptly stopped, trickling pixie dust on Alex's head and causing her to sneeze harshly. The pixie floated down in front of Alex. She was roughly as long as Alex's hand and seemed to be about Alex's age. Her hair was cut short and she wore the white of a new recruit, although her armor had floral touches. She smiled at Alex as her skin seemed to glow. "Hey, I haven't seen you here before," the pixie exclaimed. "My name is Jollies!"

Jollies twirled in the air and curtsied politely. Alex laughed at the enchanting young pixie. "I'm Alex, pleased to meet you."

"Are you eating all by yourself?"

"Yeah, well, I'm sort of new here. I didn't know who to sit with."

Jollies skittered around Alex's head and asked, "Mind if I join you?" Jollies landed on Alex's shoulder before she could answer and pulled out a small sandwich. "I haven't seen a human in the program before. Didn't think you could ride dragons, to be honest."

Alex straightened up. She wasn't sure if she was comfortable enough for Jollies. "I was told I'm the first one," Alex explained. "We can ride dragons, but Myrddin told me we have a steeper learning curve."

"You got to meet Myrddin? That must be why you're here. Sounds like you might be a little bit special for a human."

"Why? Didn't you meet him when you were recruited?"

Jollies stretched out her wings, and one of them tickled Alex's cheek. "Nope. I don't think anyone has," she answered. "But that's probably because there are lots of pixies in the dragonriders."

"I hope you don't think this is rude, but I didn't know pixies could ride dragons. Aren't they a little bit large for you?"

Jollies jumped to her feet and leapt off of Alex. Alex winced, expecting to be slapped for upsetting the pixie. She remembered what she'd read about them in Peter Pan—only room enough for one emotion.

But Jollies was beaming.

Literally.

She flew close to Alex's face. "Yeah, you would think, right?" Jollies exclaimed. "Turns out they've been breeding a special dragon just for us pixies. Super small, and they're used for special recon missions. I would die to be part of the Hairballs crew. Oh, I'd friggin' die to ride with them. They're so cool, and they've been on all sorts of insane missions, and they only accept the best pixie riders."

Jollies stopped talking and held her hand over her mouth as she blushed. Her whole body turning bright red. "I'm sorry, sometimes I rant when I get too excited."

Alex giggled and waved away Jollies' worries. "Don't worry about it," she said. "I think it's pretty cute. So, it's an all-pixie squad?"

"Yep, and it's the only one like it. It's mostly because we're so small. I'm pretty sure if you found a way to shrink yourself, you could join. Their motto is 'Size doesn't matter, talent does.' But, I mean, you kinda have to be tiny to get on the dragon, so maybe size does matter. Either way, it's gonna be me who sets the Dark One's ass on fire with the fury of my dragon."

Alex took a bite of her mashed potatoes. They tasted like home but not as good. As she put down her spoon, she caught the drow staring at her. "What's up with them?" Alex asked, jerking her head in the direction of the drow and the gnome.

Jollies looked at the duo, trying to remain as inconspicuous as possible. "Oh, them." Jollies sighed. "The drow is Gill Lowborn, and the surname says it all. The gnome is Brath Gimbel. They think they're tough guys is all. Ask them, and they'll tell you how they're going to be the next big heroes of the war."

"They seem like dicks."

"Ignore them. They're just stupid kids who like to pick fights."

Manny floated over to Alex and said, "I'm going to go grab seconds. You'll be okay for a little bit?" he asked. "Because of, you know." He winked a couple of his eyes at her.

Alex nodded and shooed Manny away. "Yeah, I'll be okay for a couple of minutes, don't worry."

As Manny walked away, Alex's eyesight started to fade until it was completely gone. This time, it wasn't a shock; she was prepared to descend into her personal darkness. It almost felt comfortable, taking a break from the sensory overload.

Jollies' voice came from Alex's right side. "Hey, are you okay?"

Alex could smell the pixie dust floating off Jollies as she spoke. "Yeah, I'm cool," Alex replied. "Why do you ask?"

"I don't know. I just noticed you started staring like you zoned out or something."

Alex hadn't realized she probably would look a little odd if she stopped making eye contact and stared straight ahead, but she wasn't ashamed of anything. Why not tell Jollies? Alex took a quick, short breath. "Oh, it's because I'm blind," Alex explained. "When Manny leaves, I can't see."

Jollies floated to Alex's other shoulder. "Really? I've never heard of a blind dragonrider before," the pixie exclaimed. "That's so cool."

Alex's vision came back, and she saw Manny heading toward her. She also saw Gill and Brath stand up and make their way over. *Just great*, Alex thought.

Gill pulled up a seat across from Alex, his purple eyes dancing. "Wait a minute," he said. His voice was far too gruff for a child's. It sounded like he'd been smoking a pipe his whole life. "Did you just say you're blind?"

Alex sat up straight and pushed her tray to the side. "Yeah, I did say I was blind. What of it?"

Brath scoffed as he burst out laughing. "What the hell are *you* going to do, then?" he mocked. "You can't see anything without your seeing-eye Beholder. You planning on hitting the Dark One with your cane?"

Alex went red and she felt her heart rate increase. She hadn't expected anyone here to make fun of her for being blind. She almost didn't know what to say, but she did know she wasn't going to back down. "I got into the program, didn't I?" she shot back. "And I did it without being able to see. Think that speaks for itself."

Brath cracked his knuckles as he took another step toward Alex. "Looks to me like things are bad enough with the Dark One that we have to start accepting cripples."

Alex jumped to her feet, nearly knocking over her food. "Who the hell are you calling a cripple?" she shouted.

Brath looked like he was going to back down for a second as he cast a glance at Gill, who merely shrugged and looked disinterested after his initial teasing. "I'm calling *you* a cripple," Brath reiterated. "You're probably gonna be the first one to get smoked. You humans are weak and lazy anyway, even when you have both your eyes, which you don't."

Brath took off his jacket and tossed it over Manny, covering all of Manny's eyes.

Everything went black. Alex immediately got disoriented and instinctively reached in front of her to grab something. She nearly lost her balance but managed to regain it quickly. She didn't dare move, though.

Brath's nasal voice cut through the darkness. "Exactly," Brath spat. "What's to keep me from blackening those smug, useless human eyes?"

Gill's voice was the next one Alex heard. "Come on, Brath, cut it out," he said. "She's had enough."

"I'm just saying, why the hell do we need this dead weight? Just our luck, we'll end up having to risk our necks for her."

Finally, Alex's vision came rushing back to her. She looked around to see what had happened. Manny was struggling to get the jacket off. His lack of arms wasn't doing him any favors. Jollies had flown down to him and was trying to help.

Alex stood there awkwardly. Her heart raced so fast she couldn't speak. Her eyes jumped from Brath's condescending face to Gill's indifferent gaze before she stormed off without saying a word.

The farther Alex got from Manny, the more her vision deteriorated. She walked closer to the wall as her eyesight faded, and she descended into familiar darkness with her throat tight from anger. Her hands trembled as she clenched them into fists, and she wished she'd punched Brath's face.

CHAPTER SEVEN

A lex stumbled down the hallway. She wished she could
see the crystal splendor around her, but at the same
time, she never wanted to see anything again. Brath's and
Gill's sneering faces were seared into her memory. She'd
heard derision before. Seeing it was a whole new thing.

Reflexively, Alex reached out to feel what was in front of
her. She wished she had her cane so she could have at least
some semblance of normalcy. Then she got an idea. In
Middang3ard, you could access your inventory through
your HUD.

The inventory provided at the start of the game always
had the bare minimum of equipment for each class. Hope-
fully, the HUD she had in real life wasn't any different.

She tapped the nodes on her temples and heard them
hum to life. If she'd had Manny nearby, she would have seen
the holographic interface that stretched from one temple to
the other, covering her eyes. Even though Alex couldn't see
the HUD interface, she thought she would take a gamble.

"Walking cane," Alex whispered.

Alex waited for a few seconds, feeling dumber each

second. It was probably asking too much for Myrddin to have planned this far ahead. That thought was dispelled when Alex felt the familiar weight in her hand.

Alex reached out with her cane and tapped the wall. The slight clack practically echoed in her ear. *I don't need Manny or his stupid eyes,* she thought. *I don't need any of them. There's nothing wrong with me. Idiots. Jerks.*

Alex made her way down the hall, although she had no idea where she was going. It didn't matter. She just wanted to get as far away from the source of embarrassment as she could, but she knew she couldn't run, not from this.

Alex had grown up listening to the snickers of other children. She'd always thought that was why her parents had decided to homeschool her—they assumed she wasn't strong enough to deal with the other children—but she'd always believed they'd done her a disservice.

Strength was something Alex had in spades. She'd used her strength in *Middang3ard* VR for some time. It was a strength the rest of her party and anyone she came across could attest to.

This was different, though. This stung more than Alex could ever have imagined. Anytime someone poked fun at her before, she could always chalk it up to that person's ignorance. Not like this.

Brath was right. What was a blind girl doing trying to ride a dragon?

What if the magic Myrddin was creating didn't work? What if she was going to have to go back home with her tail between her legs and always aware she'd come this close to experiencing something amazing but had not been able to grasp it?

An interesting smell hit Alex's nose, something she hadn't run into before, not like the flowers in the garden. This was different. It wasn't even remotely familiar. Alex figured she might as well check it out. She had no idea where she was anyway.

She was glad to be back in the dark. Her thoughts were clearer without the light, without everything moving around her, without feeling the need to look at everything. It was weird. She'd never felt like this when she'd been playing VR.

After Alex logged off VR, she'd always felt a slight sense of relief, along with a tinge of sadness. She had not been sad she couldn't see anymore. Right now, Alex would give anything to be back home and never see this place again.

She continued down the hallway and listened to the way the crystals moved around her. She could practically hear them rubbing against each other. As she walked, she wondered what the smell she was chasing could be and gave herself over to the search.

This wasn't any different from a game her mother used to play with her when she was a kid. It had been one of her favorite cooking games. Liza would hide a piece of fruit or a vegetable somewhere in the kitchen. Alex would then come into the kitchen and try to sniff it out.

After a while, the kitchen wasn't big enough for the game, and they expanded it into the living room. When the living room became too small, they included upstairs. Soon it was the entire house, and after that, outside as well.

After a few months, Alex could name nearly every spice, every fruit, every ingredient, one by one, just from one whiff. She used to pretend she was the main character from the book *Perfume*, minus the creepy serial-killer parts of the story.

She never quite developed a strong enough sense of smell to build entire worlds in her imagination, but she knew she had a gift. It was this gift that was guiding her through the halls of the Wasp's Nest.

As Alex walked, she tried to catalog each of the new

scents she came across. They weren't exactly new, though. She'd smelled them since she first arrived. They were the scents of elves or gnomes or the crystal walls. Still, there was one unique aroma that stood out amongst them all, and the source was what she searched for.

Alex tapped her cane against the wall until she could tell there was a corner. She swung her cane out in front slowly to avoid hitting anyone walking by. The hallway seemed empty enough, so she stepped out and turned the corner.

A soft voice popped into Alex's head. *There you go. You're almost there.*

Alex screamed and jumped back as she dropped her cane. "Who's there?" she asked as she bent over to find her cane.

Alex knew the difference between someone speaking to her when she wasn't aware and being alone. This was different. This felt like it was a thought in her head, but it wasn't her thought.

Don't be frightened, child. Just a little farther. Take the left up here.

Alex felt for her cane and grabbed it. She stood up and tapped until she was closer to the wall. "Why should I trust you? Who are you?" Alex asked as she tried to keep her voice from trembling.

Do you not have a sense of adventure, Child of Dust?

This was the second time Alex had been challenged today. The first time had stirred her anger. This time it was irritating. Why was everyone so intent on calling her out as if they had any idea what she was capable of. "What makes you think I don't?" Alex challenged.

The voice laughed, a deep, growling, almost warm sound. *It's just that you've asked so many questions so far. I've rarely seen an adventurer take the time to inquire of everything that is currently happening.*

"I wouldn't make a very good adventurer if I blindly

walked into every trap laid in front of me, would I? I'm pretty sure that would just make me a dead adventurer."

The voice laughed again. Whoever was speaking to Alex was obviously amused. *Good answer, Dustling, good answer.* The voice chuckled. *I can assure you Myrddin has not placed anything in the Wasp's Nest that would truly wish to harm you. Why would he bring you here, just to cause your death?*

"You got a point there. All right, lead the way."

Turn left here and take the hall all the way down. I'll be waiting for you.

Alex did as she was told. She could hear the crystals shifting around her, and the unfamiliar smell was getting stronger and stronger. Finally, her cane tapped against a dead end. She pressed her hand to the freakishly warm crystal. "Is this it?" Alex asked.

The voice came bubbling back up in Alex's head. *Imagine the door opening,* the voice instructed. *See it opening before you and come visit with me so we may speak in person.*

Alex thought of the door to her room swinging open. There was a dull green sky outside, and she could see her neighborhood.

The crystal against Alex's hand started to shift and change, pulling itself back to reveal an empty space. She tapped her cane in front of her to double-check, then stepped into the space.

The room was filled with the unfamiliar and overwhelming scent. Whatever she had smelled dominated and was hot as well, almost the kind of heat you get from someone breathing too heavily over you.

The voice was back in Alex's head. *Come closer, Dustling, so I may see you better. Come, sit and talk with me. I wish to know you better.*

Alex tapped across the floor, getting closer to the scent. "Why did you want to meet with me?" she asked.

There is something different about you. Different than the rest. I wished to see what it is.

Alex snorted derisively. "Yeah, you could say something's different." She sighed. "I don't think I belong here, not like everyone else."

A huff of hot air blasted Alex in the face. The heat in the room must have just been turned on, and the air had a musty scent to it. *Who is to say who belongs in war?* the voice asked. *War is not a particularly natural state. Perhaps none of us belong here.*

"What do you mean?"

The Dark One marches on Middang3ard, and we have gathered here, away from our families, children sitting amongst the ancients. But perhaps you are too fragile for this war. Some of us are born of steel, to be molded by the fire. Others are born of glass and crystal, to be marveled at from afar.

"I'm not a fragile piece of glass."

The voice laughed again in Alex's head. It sounded genuine and caring. *Dustling, may I ask a favor of you?* the voice inquired. *I wish to know you better.*

Alex squirmed uncomfortably. The straightforwardness of her interrogator was slightly disconcerting. "Okay, what do you want to know?" she asked.

I'd like to read your memories and understand your experiences to gauge how fragile or strong you are. I see so much fragility, yet so much strength.

"My memories? How are you going to do that?"

I have my ways.

Alex wrung her hands on her cane. "I don't know how I feel about you mucking around in my mind."

The voice laughed uproariously. *I am already mucking about*, the voice replied. *But I do not pry where I am unwanted.*

Alex sighed as she thought it over. This voice was obviously in her head, which meant it was speaking to her telepathically. What would the harm be in letting it see a couple of memories? It wasn't like she'd led a particularly interesting life. "All right," Alex said reluctantly. "Go ahead and take a look."

There was a long period of silence, the unfamiliar room filling up more and more with the scent. *"Oh, yes. So this is the real you,"* the voice murmured.

With those words, Alex felt the world around her slipping away. She had the distinct feeling of falling, and then there was nothing.

CHAPTER EIGHT

When Alex could see again, there were clouds all around her. She wasn't sure where she was, though. It felt as if she were looking at herself in a mirror or a dream. She could see her body while she was in it, and it was extremely disorienting.

As she looked around, she noticed she was surrounded by dragons and dragonriders. She realized she was in the air, and this was a place she'd been before. This wasn't happening right now. This was a memory of some mission she'd played in *Middang3ard* VR.

Jim was at Alex's side. He was smiling and waving to get her attention. The rest of her party was lined up behind him, and there were more dragonriders she didn't recognize as well. It looked like they were on a raid with a couple of other groups.

Alex wracked her brain to try to figure out exactly what the mission was and what they were doing. She also absent-mindedly wondered how she'd gotten here. Her brain felt fuzzy, and it was difficult to put thoughts together. The only thing that seemed right was watching events unfold as if they were a movie, which made much more sense.

Jim shouted at Alex over the wind, "Hey, I did some research on these frost giants before we came out here. They don't look like they're going to be too tough. We got this. Real easy."

Alex watched herself speaking, the words coming from her mouth even though she wasn't thinking them. It was a freaky experience. "They can't be too easy," she replied. "This raid is two levels higher than I am. I highly doubt this is going to be simple."

One of the riders behind Alex pushed his dragon up farther, so he was between Alex and Jim. "What are you two talking about?" he asked. "Trying to keep secrets? You know this raid isn't going to work if we aren't communicating with each other."

A rider behind them shouted, "What's there to communicate? We're going up against frost giants. We're riding fire-breathing dragons, or at least anyone who got the memo has a dragon that breathes fire. Thank God no one brought any frost dragons. This'll be over before lunch."

The voice that had spoken to Alex before bubbled up in her head again. *You seem to be nervous in this memory,* the voice mused. *Just relax. Talk to me. Don't worry about trying to do or say the right thing. As long as you relax, the memory will flow naturally.*

Alex didn't see the point in arguing. Obviously, the voice knew more about reliving memories than she did, and it sounded kind of nice to sit back and watch her previous exploits. Maybe she could learn something new by watching.

The host of dragonriders soared higher. As Alex relaxed, the emotions she'd felt that day washed over her. She'd been apprehensive; something had been off with the mission description.

Alex pulled up her HUD and looked at the description of the mission.

A group of frost giants has stolen the long-lost scrolls of El-Zeroth. They have hidden them deep within their fortress. It is up to you to retrieve the scrolls to keep the

frost giants of Nordom from reading the hidden secrets of the scrolls.

Alex reread the raid description. On the surface, there didn't seem to be anything odd, other than that this was a raid given specifically to dragonriders, which would be like creating a mermaid-specific mission for water mages.

It would be too easy.

The dragonriders clustered together to speak about their plan for taking on the frost giants. Most of the riders thought it would be best to hit the giants straight on. They could easily burn through their defenses. Frost giants always built their defenses out of ice. It would be a slaughter.

Alex kept her opinion to herself, which caught Jim's attention. Usually, she was one of the first to put her ideas forward. She didn't care much if people listened to them since she knew the mission was most important, and having more ideas flowing meant better planning.

In the distance, Alex could see the frost giants' fortress. It was built into a snowy mountain ridge and looked like it was carved completely out of ice. It produced the sweeping awe of a Victorian mansion, looking far too sophisticated.

Alex thought about everything she knew about frost giants. She had the odd feeling someone was listening to her thoughts but pushed the worry away. This was supposed to play out like a movie or something. She was just along for the ride.

Frost giants came from an entirely different realm. They weren't native to Middang3ard and had come to this realm with the Norse gods. Loki had brought them here in the last released expansion.

The raid before this had involved helping Thor win a battle against Loki, effectively locking all the frost giants back into their realm. According to the in-game lore, there shouldn't have been frost giants in Middang3ard anymore, and that was what was off.

She flew closer to Jim and waved him over. "I don't think we should strike them head-on."

Jim sighed, rolled his shoulders back, and sat down on his dragon. "Why not?"

"Frost giants aren't even supposed to be in the game right now, remember? We all did that Thor and Loki raid. We sent them back. Whatever stole those scrolls isn't a proper frost giant. They're up to something weird."

"So, you're saying we should split up and let everyone else have all the fun?"

Alex was already messaging the rest of the players in the raid. She had a feeling none of them were going to take her seriously. Everyone seemed pretty gung-ho to take on the giants. She couldn't really blame them; giants netted a lot of XP.

But Alex wasn't that shortsighted.

Killing enemies gave XP, but it was nowhere near the XP and loot you got from completing a mission without dying, which was what Alex was after.

In a couple of minutes, Alex received messages from the other players. As expected, none were interested in detouring from the original plan. Everyone thought they had the battle won.

Alex wrote another message to her party.

I really think they're making a mistake. I think we're going to get wiped out by whatever the fake frost giants have in store. We should take another route. Go around back. See if we can swipe the scrolls that way. The mission doesn't say anything about killing the giants, just getting the scrolls back.

Jim messaged Alex.

They're on an enormous mountain of ice. Why wouldn't they be frost giants?

Because Frost Giants are subterranean. Why would they build anything on a mountain?

You got a point there. So, we're going around the back?

Don't you think it's kind of messed up to let everyone else just get wiped out?

I sent them all the same message I sent you guys. Besides, we don't know for sure. We could be wrong and fly into something even worse. We'll find out when we get there.

Alex and her party broke away from the rest of the dragonriders. No one from the other parties noticed or cared. The mountain came up quickly as Alex's party swooped to the right to take the long way around.

To say the mountain was huge would be to minimize its sheer size. It was roughly the width of a small island. It looked like a continent had been ripped from the ocean and stretched toward the sky. It was impossible to see the top.

The party had been flying for nearly fifteen minutes, still trying to reach the opposite side of the mountain, the polar opposite of the original coordinates.

Phillis, who was riding a swap-in dragon for her ice dragon, crossed her arms. "Am I the only one who is insanely bored?" she whined. "If I wanted to just ride around, I wouldn't have joined a raid."

Alex looked at Phillis with disbelief. "Honestly, how can you be bored right now?"

"Everyone else is off doing some major killing, and we're just floating around like a couple of pigeons."

Alex leaned forward, and her dragon anchor glowed brightly as she sped past the rest of her party members. How could you possibly be bored up here? she wondered.

The bubbling voice of her invisible friend came through her thoughts again. *My thoughts exactly*, the voice agreed. *I don't think your friends have the same appreciation for the skies as you do.*

Alex knew the voice was right, but she still felt the need to defend her friends. "Not everyone plays *Middang3ard* for the same reasons," she said. "I kind of latched onto riding dragons as soon as I found out you could. Some people like the fighting, I guess. I love the flying."

The voice chuckled. *That's good to know.*

Up ahead of Alex, at the new coordinates, was a swarm of black. She flipped down her HUD to zoom in so she could get a better view. The black swarm was made up of giant ravens. While the birds were nearly half the size of the dragons, they were still only ravens.

Alex hit the radio on her HUD and shouted, "Looks like you guys will see some excitement after all!"

She sped toward the congress of ravens. She'd always thought "congress" was such a cool name for a group of birds, almost as good as a murder of crows.

The rest of the party caught up with Alex because she slowed down to give them a chance to get some kills in.

Jim swept into the mass of ravens as his dragon launched fire from its mouth and burned through the first line of birds easily. He mimed pulling back on his reins, causing his dragon to come to a full stop before spinning in a circle and burning everything in sight.

The rest of the dragonriders tore into the congress as well. Their elemental dragons filled the air with the crackle of lightning or boulders they flung.

Alex held back and watched the battle before her. She knew they wouldn't need her help and was content to enjoy the still sky around her.

The invisible voice made itself known again. *Why didn't you join the fight?* the voice asked.

Alex was roused from her peaceful thoughtfulness. "Huh. Oh, I don't know," she said. "It's kinda nice over here, and I was questing all day. I don't need the XP. I just wanted to figure out what was going on with the raid, and I was curious about what's up with the whole scroll thing."

After Alex's party cleared away the ravens, she flew through the shower of black feathers to where her HUD's coordinates were pointing her. Alex could see there was a doorway built into the side of the mountain. It wasn't locked and only had a latch. "Bingo," she said as she got close enough to pull the door open.

Alex's HUD binged. It was a message from some of the other players. Turned out they had all been wiped out. The frost giants hadn't been giants at all. It looked like it was an illusion by the god Loki.

Jim flew over to Alex as they both dismounted their dragons and jumped through the door into the mountain. "Looks like you were right," he admitted. "Sorry for doubting you."

Alex selected a lantern from her inventory. "Jim, I'd be worried if you did everything I said," she admitted. "I appreciate your judgment. Keeps me from thinking I'm always right."

For the first time since Alex had heard the voice in her head, she reached out to it to say something. "I can't wait to show you what we found," she exclaimed. "It was really..."

Suddenly her thoughts became fuzzy again. The world around her was breaking up, and she had the same sensation of falling, followed by a loud voice repeating something over and over. This voice was not coming from her head; it was very real.

Alex's eyesight returned. She looked around, confused as to where she was. Manny was floating in front of her, some of his eyes glaring and the others wide open. "What the hell are you doing in here?" the Beholder demanded.

Alex stood up and prepared to brush past Manny. She'd completely forgotten she'd stormed away from the mess hall because of her argument with Brath. "I'm okay," she said briskly.

"You aren't supposed to be in here yet," Manny continued.

"Why not? What's so important in here?"

Alex turned, and the blood drained from her face as her heart rate doubled.

Crouched before Alex was a smooth-skinned ether dragon. It looked as if it didn't have any scales and was a mixture of different shades of green. As the dragon leaned forward, its green skin shimmered to white and then purple, making it look as if it were liquid. The dragon was smaller than any Alex had seen in *Middang3ard*.

Alex backed away out of instinct. Now she knew what that strange smell was: the scent of a real dragon. *Nice to meet you, Alex,* the voice said in her head. *My name is Chine.*

"Nice to m-meet you," Alex stammered, raising her hand weakly.

One of Manny's tentacles wrapped around her wrist and pulled her away from the dragon. "Come on, we need to get going," he barked as he rushed Alex out of the room.

CHAPTER NINE

Manny didn't say much as he ushered Alex out of the room and down the hall. They walked for some time before Alex finally cracked and spoke first. "Those guys were jerks," Alex said softly. "I know I shouldn't have gotten that upset, but I couldn't be around them."

Manny hardly seemed to notice what Alex said. "Oh, I don't care about you leaving," Manny finally admitted. "You're a big girl, and I have no doubt you can take care of yourself. I was supposed to keep you away from the dragon's nest, though. Myrddin was very specific about that."

Alex smiled at Manny. "Well, how about you keep my little secret, and I'll keep yours?"

Manny's eyes checked over his shoulder to see if there was anyone around. "All right, deal," he whispered. "Now, let's get you to your room before anyone notices you're not around."

They started down the hall again. "Wait, 'my room?'" Alex asked, "Am I going to be living here?"

"Think of it as an introduction to living in a dorm room

in college, except you only have one roommate, and I don't think she takes up much space.

Manny turned a corner, and the crystal opened a door into a room. The number 12 was above it. "Here you go," he said. "Go ahead and get settled in. I'll be back when it's time for the binding ceremony."

"The binding ceremony? What's that?"

A mischievous grin spread over Manny's huge face. "Oh, come on, don't you like surprises?" he asked before spinning around and racing down the hall, cackling like a madman.

Alex couldn't help chuckling. That was the most eldritch thing she'd seen Manny do, and even so, it was far too good-natured to be the action of a true eldritch creature.

The room Alex stood in now was very different from those she'd seen in the Wasp's Nest so far. First, the crystal had a different appearance, more like redwood. If Alex looked closely, she could still see it was crystal. This must have been to create more of a homey feel rather than the grandiose nature of the rest of the Nest. Alex was thankful for it.

She walked farther into the room as her vision started to dim. It didn't disappear completely, though. Manny must have decided to give her some space but not get far enough away to blind her.

The room was modestly furnished. There was a desk, a rocking chair, and a bed built into the wall. Alex scratched her head as she spun to look at the room. She could have sworn Manny had said something about having a roommate, but there wasn't any other furniture.

She sat down on her bed and wondered where her room-mate's furniture could be. Then she noticed it. There was a small bed on her dresser, barely the size of her cellphone. A miniature dresser was next to the bed. *Guess I'm rooming with a pixie,* Alex thought. Might as well rest until she gets here.

The bed was soft enough that she sprawled out and was asleep within minutes.

ALEX WOKE to the sound of someone singing softly and sat upright as fast as she could. She was slightly confused as to where she was before remembering everything that had happened over the last couple of days. She swung around and hung her feet off the bed.

She noticed someone brought the bags her mom had sent ahead into the room and stacked them by the dresser, mostly books. It would be interesting to read braille even though she could see.

The soft singing stopped, and Alex heard a flutter of wings just before she smelled pixie dust. Jollies flew from the desk and stopped in front of Alex's face while beaming brightly. "Oh, good, you're awake," the pixie exclaimed. "I've been waiting for you to wake up forever!"

Alex returned the enthusiastic smile and scooted down her bed so she could lean against the wall and get out of Jollies' brightness. "Glad to see you too," Alex said. "Looks like I'm going to be your roommate."

"Good. I haven't had a roommate since I got here. Everyone else has been all buddy-buddy with their roommates, and I've just been hanging out with the other pixies, trying to make friends. Everyone is so cliquish, it's ridiculous."

"Yeah, I guess so."

"So, how do you like the Wasp's Nest so far?"

Alex told Jollies everything that had been on her mind since she arrived. How enthralled she was with the magic and tech everywhere. She told the pixie this was the first time she'd ever really seen magic, and she hadn't been expecting it to be part of the architecture.

Jollies had a similar feeling. Where she was from, magic wasn't used for mundane things. Magic was reserved for formal occasions and events. It was weird to see magic being used for something as simple as a building, but she liked it.

As the two of them talked, Alex's mind started to drift back to Chine. Alex had only briefly seen Chine, but she still couldn't believe she'd actually talked to a dragon. She couldn't wrap her head around how much personality Chine had compared to the dragons she'd met in *Middang3ard*.

"Hey, Jollies? Have you met any dragons since you've been here?"

Jollies floated down and sat next to Alex on the bed. "Met a dragon? Not in person. Not yet. We're supposed to be doing that tonight," she answered.

"So, you haven't spoken to one yet?"

"Nope. Why are you asking?"

"No reason."

Jollies fidgeted as she sat. "Hey, I wanted to apologize for earlier," she started. "About Gill and Brath. That was out of line. Brath is...well, Brath kinda hates humans. He's still really upset they didn't come to help when the gnome realm was attacked."

Alex looked up. "What happened to the gnome realm?"

"A lot of them were wiped out, and those who weren't were enslaved. The remaining gnomes—the ones who are still alive—are either all part of MERC or the military."

"Oh, my God, that's awful. I can see why he has an issue with us. Do you know why the humans didn't help?"

"I'm not that into politics. Plus, no one really knows why it took the humans so long to join the fight. You're here now, though, and that's all that matters. And if Brath or Gill try that crap again, I got your back."

A loud gong came from the room's speaker system. Alex and Jollies jumped at the noise, but Jollies quickly composed herself and started zipping around the room. "All right, finally!" she shouted. "It's time to go! Don't forget your dragon anchor!"

Alex got off the bed and checked to see if her dragon anchor was still around her wrist. "Go where?" she asked as she followed Jollies out of the room.

Jollies cast a glance over her shoulder, smiling from ear to ear. "It's time for the binding!"

CHAPTER TEN

Jollies and Alex met Manny outside their room and he led them to what Jollies called the Dragons' Nest. Alex could smell the now-familiar scent of Chine, mixed with what Alex now knew was other dragons.

Manny answered the slew of questions Jollies asked. Alex wasn't paying attention because she had a rough idea of what the binding ceremony was. She was more concerned with how Myrddin was going to grant her eyesight.

As the three of them walked down the hall toward the Dragons' Nest, Gill and Brath stepped out of their room directly in front of them. Brath didn't waste any time filling the air with animosity. He didn't even need to speak. Alex could feel the hatred rolling off the gnome.

Gill didn't seem to have the same ill will, though. He looked at Alex with an air of indifference, and Alex was surprised when he spoke to her. "Did you two get called to the binding ceremony as well?"

Alex numbly nodded. "Yeah, we heard a gong," she muttered.

"Guess we're going to be in the same training class."

Brath walked past Gill and the rest of them. "Great, I get to watch the human fail," he growled.

Alex felt anger well up but squashed it down quickly. She remembered what Jollies had said about Brath's home realm. If this was how he had to vent his frustration, Alex could be understanding until she got to know him better.

Rather than follow Brath, Gill fell in with Jollies, Manny, and Alex. He didn't say anything as he walked alongside them, and Alex was reminded of a shadow—a mysterious, handsome shadow. Alex tried not to stare at Gill but felt herself blushing.

Brath apparently knew the way to the Nest because he didn't stay close enough to follow Manny's instructions. He rounded corner after corner ahead of them while Jollies turned her questioning to Gill. Alex paid closer attention to their conversation than she had to Manny's and Jollies', but she wasn't able to catch much.

Finally, they came to a cathedral-style door. This must have been the one Alex had tapped with her cane the first time she came through. Brath reached for the door, and a panel formed from the crystal and stretched toward him. He pressed his hand to the surface, and the majestic double doors opened to the Dragons' Nest.

The Nest felt larger than the last time Alex was here. Although she hadn't seen much of it, she knew it was nothing like what was in front of her now. It opened directly in front of a staircase that went nearly to the ceiling. Along the staircase were crystal rails. At the top was a platform where Myrddin stood.

As the four potential dragonriders started up the steps, hissing and roaring filled the room. No one spoke, but Jollies hummed nervously. When they got to the top, Myrddin bowed politely to each and motioned for them to look over the side of the platform.

Four dragons sat beneath them. They were as large as the ones she'd seen in *Middang3ard*. She'd had no idea there was so much room under the stairs.

Myrddin pointed and said, "Timber, an earth dragon." Looking at the four, Alex saw a large dragon curled in the corner of the holding pen. Its skin was the color of moist, fertile earth, and its horns were smaller than the rest of the dragons'. The texture of its wings could have been mistaken for bark, and as it yawned, its body shimmered in and out of sight.

"Next is Amber, an electric dragon." This one was noticeably smaller than the rest, but not as small as Chine. It flitted back and forth with nervous energy. Its scales were steely-blue, and electricity crackled between them. The sweeping horns on its long face looked like conducting rods with bolts of lighting shooting between them.

"And now we have Furi, a fire dragon." Furi took up most of the space in the pen. It was the largest of all the dragons, and its chest was covered in golden scales that looked like coins. Massive, sweeping horns stretched from its head nearly to its shoulders. The dragon had rippling biceps and a muscular chest.

"And finally, Chine, our only ether dragon." Chine crouched in the opposite corner. His scales shifted between different colors. He was the only dragon who looked at Alex as she stared over the platform. *Ah, Alex,* Chine said telepathically. *I'm glad to see you were one of the four chosen.*

Alex was about to respond when she felt Myrddin's hand on her shoulder. "Come, Alex," he said. "The binding ceremony is about to begin." Myrddin turned to the other three teenagers. "Please line up shoulder to shoulder from smallest to largest."

Jollies zipped over to Brath's right side before anyone had a chance to say anything. Gill and Alex sized each other up, and Alex smiled awkwardly as she stood at Gill's left side since she was nearly a head taller than him.

Myrddin spread his arms wide. "Let the binding begin!" he shouted.

The room was filled with silence. Nothing happened.

Chine's voice surfaced in Alex's head. *Exciting, isn't it?* He laughed.

Alex reached out to Chine with her own thoughts. *Chine, is it?* she asked.

Yes, Alex?

What exactly is happening?

Alex leaned forward to get a look at what everyone else was doing. Jollies had her eyes closed tightly, and Brath was tapping his feet impatiently. Gill was the only one who seemed to be unconcerned about what was happening.

Chine's voice pierced Alex's thoughts. *The dragons are choosing their riders. They're each speaking with a rider right now, same as I am doing with you. Going through their memories, trying to find who they're most compatible with.*

Alex nodded and realized she probably looked crazy. "You guys choose us, we don't choose you," she murmured.

Exactly. Oh, I think we have our first one.

The dragon Timber spread his wings, flapped once, and soared into the air. He stared into Gill's eyes for some time before turning to Myrddin and nodding.

Myrddin stepped forward and grabbed Gill's wrist, the wrist with the dragon anchor. He whispered something under his breath, and Gill's dragon anchor began to glow the same color as Timber's eyes. Timber breathed out a spiral of fire that engulfed Gill.

Alex screamed and leapt backward as the flames swallowed the elf. When the flames went out, Gill was still standing but was holding his chest and breathing heavily.

Gill looked up at Timber, who only nodded before flying

toward the ceiling. The crystal separated, allowing Timber to fly out into the night sky.

Myrddin rested his hand on Gill's shoulder. "You may wait outside," he said. "You've been bound."

Gill did as Myrddin said. He was shaking slightly as he walked, but other than that, he seemed to be perfectly fine. *Would have been nice if someone had warned him,* Alex thought.

Chine's laughter rippled through Alex's mind. *It wouldn't be much of a ceremony if everyone knew the details.*

Amber rose into the air. Electricity crackled, and the hair on the back of Alex's neck stood up. The dragon floated toward Jollies and met the pixie's eyes. A bolt of lightning crackled from above and struck the spot where Jollies hovered.

Once the smoke dispersed, Alex saw that Jollies was still floating, although her hair looked like she'd stuck her finger in an electrical outlet. She turned to Alex with a shaky smile.

Myrddin walked over to Amber and nodded.

Amber shrank in size. It happened so fast Alex could hardly tell what was going on. The dragon was now roughly the size of a large cat as it took off into the sky.

Alex leaned over to check on the two remaining dragons. *Looks like those two will be a good match,* Chine mused. *They both seem to want to fly very fast.*

Next, Furi spread his oversized wings and flapped once, sending a gust of wind through the whole room. The fire dragon glared at Brath as the dragon's lips trembled. Alex wasn't sure if the dragon was going to breathe fire or bite off Brath's head.

Brath didn't back down or show any fear. Instead, he stepped up to the dragon until they were nose to nose at the edge of the platform. Brath raised his dragon anchor and it glowed a deep, blood red, the same color as Furi's eyes.

Chine's voice echoed in Alex's head. *They've got a good*

amount of anger and hatred between them, he said. *I hope they don't burn each other.*

Furi snarled and spat a fireball at Brath's feet. The fireball exploded and covered the gnome in flames. Brath stood there until the flames passed. He coughed as he inhaled smoke. Furi smiled as he took off into the sky. Brath left the room and gave Alex side-eye while he said, "Guess the human gets the runty leftover."

Chine rose into the air and looked into Alex's eyes. The dragon's eyes were kind. They looked old and reminded Alex of her grandmother's. *Hardly*, Chine thought to Alex. *Myrddin and I decided it would be best if we saved you for last. Our binding will be a little more complicated.*

Myrddin stepped forward and nodded. "You two bonded earlier today while you were sharing memories," he said. "Before we perform the spell, we need to bind you technologically. Please raise your dragon anchor."

Alex did as she was told, and her anchor glowed the same color as Chine's eyes. "With that taken care of, we'll do the spell. Alex, I can't heal your eyes, but I *can* give you Chine's sight. It won't be the same as with Manny. You will be able to see, no matter how far away you are from the dragon. But I must warn you, a dragon's sight is a thousand times more powerful than a human's. It might be a strain. Do you understand?"

Alex didn't care how difficult it was going to be. She would have given both her arms to be able to ride a dragon again. She wanted to be in the sky. "Yeah, I can handle it," she said.

"All right then, let's do this."

Myrddin stood behind Alex and covered her eyes with his hand. Alex felt a warm sensation on her eyelids as she stood in darkness. Myrddin was chanting something, but Alex couldn't make it out. After a moment, the warmth started burning, then changed to searing pain.

Myrddin released Alex, and she fell forward with her right hand held over her eyes. She wanted to scream in pain, but she didn't want any of the other riders to hear. She could handle this.

Alex slowly opened her eyes. They felt heavy, as if someone had bolted them shut. The first thing she saw was Chine's eyes. They were deep purple, and then they weren't. Alex's head erupted in pain as she backed away.

Chine leaned forward to get a better look at Alex.

Alex's head was screaming from the pain. When she looked at the dragon and saw the way his scales morphed between different colors, the knocking pain behind her eyes increased. She tried to stand but suddenly became sick to her stomach. There was too much color. Too much vibrancy. She wanted it to stop. She wanted the darkness. Seeing was making her sick.

Chine sensed what was wrong and flew backward, away from Alex and closer to the shadows.

Myrddin moved behind Alex. The sound of his steps made Alex whip around. She nearly screamed when she looked at him. She could see each and every pore on his face as if she were looking through a microscope, but that wasn't all. She could see the individual threads in his clothing.

Every detail was magnified; it was too much. She couldn't stop the scream this time. Her brain was overloading. She pitched forward to keep from throwing up and covered her eyes. "Oh, my God. It hurts so much," she whimpered.

Slowly she opened her eyes, but she was still seeing too much. She felt like she could see each cell that made up her hands in excruciating detail. "Take it away," she muttered before she realized what she'd said.

Myrddin leaned down and helped prop her against the

wall. Alex shut her eyes and fought back the tears from the migraine pounding in her head. "Are you sure you can do this?" he asked.

Alex took a deep breath and imagined herself on Chine's back with the sun in her face and the wind blowing through her hair. She cracked her eyes open. The flood of visual information was almost too much. She thought she might faint, but she held on with her teeth gritted and fought through the pain. "I'm going to be a dragonrider," Alex ground out slowly. "No matter what."

Alex stood and faced Chine. She opened her eyes as wide as she could and stared into the dragon's eyes as he flew closer. His deep-purple eyes were rimmed with blue and green, which changed to yellow and orange. They held each other's gaze for some time before Chine nodded and followed the path of the other dragons out of the nest.

She watched as he flew away. When she looked at the night sky, the stars blazed with a blinding light, and she lost her balance. She hit the floor with a heavy thud and shut her eyes as tight as she could. *I'm going to fly again,* she thought, slipping in and out of consciousness. *No matter what it takes, I'm going to fly again.*

AUTHOR NOTES RAMY VANCE
JANUARY 2, 2020

"Dragons in space," that's what I said to Michael Anderle when I met him Edinburgh. "Dragons in space."

He just looked at me in that way he does, his eyes narrowed as he considered the proposal (what is refreshing about Michael is that you can play an endless game of improv with him by throwing out random terms and thoughts - to which he'll always turn it into a story).

"Will that work?" he asked me, but I knew he was already plotting.

"What's not to work? Dragons in space. Think about it. How cool would that be?"

"So you're saying this would be a second series in Middang3ard?"

"Yep."

"And what, would the dragons be wearing, what, space suits?"

Now that was a question I was prepared for: "I'm thinking mech armor and magic spells that surround their bodies with a thin layer of oxygen."

He considered this and shook his head. "We can come up with something better."

Damn it... still this was a victory. He was intrigued.

"Let me think about it," he finally said.

Over the next few days, every time I saw him, I yelled, "Dragons in space." It got to the point where if he saw me, he'd turn around and walk away. But I wasn't deterred. I just screamed all the louder: "Dragons in space!"

I think I might have oversold it. I probably didn't need to hound him. But still, it was fun. It wasn't every day you got to legitimately yell something like, "Dragons in space," at a person like Michael and get away with it.

Finally, on the last day of the conference, he nodded and said, "Dragons in space. Let's talk about it."

And from that, the Dragon Rider series was born. "Dragons in space, baby!"

PS - do me a favor. Tag Michael in a post with the hash-tag: #DragonsInSpace in the Kurtherian Gambit Group and a link to the book. It will drive him crazy, but because we're basically marketing the book, there's nothing he can do about it. (Mwahahahahaha! DRAGONS IN SPACE, BABY... DRAGONS IN FRIGGIN' SPACE!)

Thank you for reading this story!

Because of fans, I get to Research the World™, which is a pleasure, finding new locales and people to invigorate creativity so I can continue to bring you more stories.

Right now, I'm studying Hong Kong (looking at the city of Hong Kong from Hong Kong Island). It is a little cloudy, and the mountains, which are not that far away, are shrouded in mystery.

DRAGONS

I have a love/hate relationship with dragons, clearly more love than hate since I'm involved in three series right now that deal with dragons. I like that they are massive, fierce creatures with magical abilities that just look freaking cool.

I hated EVER having to role-play a fight with a dragon. I felt like I was about to become that little mess under their feet they would then wipe across the ground to get rid of.

I liked playing a Magic-User. You know, the role where we couldn't wear any decent type of armor EVER and a stupid arrow might kill us because we gained hit points at 1d4.

If this makes NO sense, it essentially means you would play a game, and when you went up a level, you threw a 4-sided die. If you rolled a 1, you gained ONE FREAKING HIT POINT per level. If you slipped on a banana peel, you could kill yourself. If a fighter (who could gain—I think—up to ten hit points, or maybe eight, per level) slipped, his friends would just laugh at his low dexterity.

So, other than admitting to my NERD qualities in a former decade, suffice it to say, dragons weren't my friends.

On the other hand, as a reader, dragons are one of the most iconic creatures in Fantasy. This guy's fears and desires for power-made-flesh in a sinuous body of armor(!) and could wield magic and fly.

@#@#%@ YOU SUPERMAN! *This was a creature of majesty!*

RAMY

So, when Ramy and I talked about doing a series of shorts (a tactical publishing decision, along with a realization about just how much time and money we had to put into a new series), he sold me when he spoke the word "dragon."

The rest of the conversation didn't matter.

He had me.

We worked through the details for the main character (always, in my opinion, the most important part of the story) as my inner NERD was squeaking *"FREAKING DRAGON!")*

If you enjoy dragon stories, LMBPN has many. Those include (already out) Sarah Noffke's *The Exceptional S. Beaufont* stories, and Kevin McLaughlin's *Steel Dragon* series. In March, I have another dragon collaboration with Martha Carr coming out, the *Dragon Trainer* series.

Jump on our email list to be told about these and the many other books we have coming your way in the future!

http://www.LMBPN.com/email

Thank you for reading our stories. It means the world to me!

Michael Anderle

Other Middang3ard Books

Never Split The Party (01)
Late To the Party (02)
It's My Party (03)
Blue Hell And Alien Fire (04)

Death Of An Author: A Middang3ard Novella

Other Books by Ramy Vance

Mortality Bites Series
Keep Evolving Series
Fatebound Series

Other Books by Michael Anderle

For a complete list of books by Michael Anderle, please visit:

www.lmbpn.com/ma-books/

All LMBPN Audiobooks are Available at Audible.com and iTunes. To see all LMBPN audiobooks, including those written by Michael Anderle please visit:

www.lmbpn.com/audible

CONNECT WITH THE AUTHORS

Connect with Ramy

Join Ramy's Newsletter

Join Ramy's FB Group: House of the GoneGod Damned!

Connect with Michael Anderle and sign up for his email list here:

Website: http://lmbpn.com

Email List: http://lmbpn.com/email/

Facebook:
www.facebook.com/TheKurtherianGambitBooks